A PLACE OF EXECUTION

*'Bastards like you dug my grave with pencils,'
Kegan snarled.* A simple thief, he was up for
life: murder was his only ticket to freedom.
The victim? Ricardo Torres. Honours graduate
of the Sorbonne, now the people's President
of a Republic steeped in the heady spirit of
revolution. Assassination, which would spark
it off, was not in Kegan's line. After years of
celibacy he was more concerned with Rojas
Modesta, but she slept with a 'tame' jaguar
named Angelito! Kegan, looking for the haven
of release beyond green hills far from the heat
and the rattle of firing squads, was pitched
into a crevasse of intrigue . . . If suspenseful
ingredients, plus a theme from today's head-
lines, make your kind of thriller, search no
further.

A PLACE OF EXECUTION

MICHAEL VINTER

A S P
Ace Stoneshire Publishing

Printed and bound in Great Britain

CONTENTS

Chaper One

FALSE CONTACT

The motion of the aircraft was making him sicker.

Not surprisingly, after eight years in the stir, his stomach rebelled against two whole bottles of Bollinger '58. None knew better than he that the long flight from Mexico City was almost over, but Nana Segovia was going as strongly as ever. Did she even stop for sleep?

'*Dear* Mr. Martinson, so *kind* to help me like this . . . it's been wonderful meeting a real gentleman, and I *do* so hope we've both enjoyed our little soiree.'

'Every minute of it.'

Bloody liar! His stomach curled. Now she was leaning closer, he wanted to puke, and he cursed her for what she'd talked him into doing. Half an hour from now, the odds were that he'd be in the hands of Customs and Excise; and there were risks enough without adding to them needlessly.

As if sensing indecision, Segovia turned on the pressure and bore down.

Charm? It was like being vamped by your own great-aunt: all teeth and golden fillings. Suddenly he wanted to plant his hand in the middle of her fat, sweaty bosom and shove her violently away; but it was even too late for that.

'Barry . . . we've come to know each other well enough for first names, haven't we? I've found there are certain people who fall into tune, spiritual tune, from the very first moment. You may not believe this,' and she paused impressively, 'but there *have* been performers I couldn't sing with, simply because we had no spiritual harmony.' A shrill, neighing laugh, and her eyes took on a thyroidal bulge. 'What a *pity* you never had voice training. You're a natural.' She patted his cheek. 'Don Jose, Escamillo: and such a *simpatico* profile!'

It was not the first time he'd been told about his profile, and by attractive women at that.

Any other time he might have laughed, but he'd gone beyond laughter, and Segovia's hard little package in his coat pocket was jabbing viciously into his left buttock. He shifted to make himself comfortable just as the no-smoking sign flickered on and people began adjusting their seat belts.

Segovia made a pettish little *tut*. An absurdly roguish flutter of grotesque eyelashes.

'Barry! Darling! Please help me ... I can never get this wretched thing quite right.'

He leaned across her lap, fumbling with the web strap; repelled by the rolls of plump thigh flesh which surged fractionally upwards to increase their contact.

She purred, 'When you come to visit me at Ciudad Felice, you may find that I know how to be very ... *grateful*.'

The champagne was affecting him disastrously; he wanted to giggle. His hand hovered fractionally above the dimpled fat knees protruding from a skirt that had 'accidentally' ridden to incredible heights. In a moment he was going to say, quite distinctly, 'If you aren't a little more discreet, madam, I shall probably reach up your drawers and twang the elastic.'

She might even like it. Rich she was, famous she

may be, but it was probably all of forty years since she'd had a masculine hand up there.

'Whatever happens,' she insisted, 'you must come to see my farewell performance. *Promise* me!'

He was saved. The aircraft slipped and tilted, to reveal through its windows the lighted airstrip of Acerrias. It also caused his ears to pop.

The clown-red lips whispered, urgently and finally, 'We mustn't be seen leaving the aircraft together. The customs ... you understand? They will turn my baggage inside out, quite definitely! But they won't bother a tourist. I wouldn't ask you to do it if there were any risk....' Once more she uttered that silly little neigh.

By the time he quit the plane Barry was exhausted, but although his headache was passing the sickness was worse. He managed to lead the queue, thus leaving Segovia to her grand exit at the top of the steps. As he walked across the powdery tarmac, swallowing to relieve the squelchy depressurization noises, he eyed the round little bottom and firm limbs of the escorting hostess with genuine appreciation. Women were something he'd really missed; an omission he intended to put right as soon as this job was over and done with.

Barry caught the foetid, warm smell of summer. Fine dust hung like a mist in starfire air; the breeze flayed the tousled palm fronds along the chainlink boundary of *Aeropuerto Acerrias*. In front of the arrivals building, the globe lights entrapped hosts of flitter moths within wan haloes.

Baggage trolleys clattered across, but Barry scarcely heard them. With every fibre stretched, the old nerve pains were there again in the arch of his rib cage, where the fear bird made its nest: he had stepped out of the night and into a scene that crawled with cameras. Flash bulbs ... *Jesus!* Already drenched with sweat, he was trembling violently. Pressmen were one thing he had to avoid at all costs.

It was Segovia, of course; her triumphal annual pilgrimage to this poxy Island Republic of San Felice. Her faithful admirers demanded it. He knew the whole story. Now he began to suspect there must exist a certain element of truth.

Desperately, Barry wiped his slimy forehead with the cuff of his sleeve.

'Your passport please?' And again, 'Señor, your passport!'

He started, shocked to his senses.

Immigration procedure; olive drab; gold braid—uniforms? He loathed them. And he loathed this fat, arrogant belly with the too ornate belt buckle. Just another kind of screw, po-faced and sneering, with a gun on the end of his chain instead of a bunch of keys.

'Tourist?' the screw inquired; and without waiting, 'Welcome to our Republic. I hope your stay here will be a happy one.'

Kegan kept his eyes down. Routine crap, said without thought; but the faked passport was getting full attention. Pursed lips, furrowed brow. The screw looked suspicious.

Without any warning at all, Barry's vision shifted. He could retaste the champagne. Staggering, he slid down the wall; then he vomited uncontrollably, and once started, never stopped until it seemed his belly had been wrung dry.

Oh, God! Now he was surrounded. He could have

scarcely attracted more attention if he'd arrived in prison dress complete with ball and chain. This was what you called stealing Segovia's thunder. She'd be furious.

'Señor Martinson! ... your passport, take it please! Are you ill, or is it just the flight? You require some water? A doctor?'

Through his haze, Barry glimpsed the anxious face of the screw, felt the passport being slipped into his hand. The air hostess was squatting beside him, too. Weak as he was, his attention wandered past the hem of her tight pulled skirt, down the stockinged curve of her thighs. She had on bright little nylon pants. Pink. His hand up there, that was more like it; suddenly he felt much better.

'The flight was turbulent,' the hostess was telling the screw. 'We had several passengers taken ill.' Her nose wrinkled at the smell of soured champagne.

Barry struggled to his feet.

'I'm better now,' he apologized. 'Thank you for all your help ... no, a doctor won't be necessary.'

Obviously, the screw was relieved. He didn't care for the smell any more than the hostess; he was anxious to be away.

'A good night's rest, Señor Martinson,' he advised. 'Get to your hotel quickly and go to bed. Air sickness will soon pass.'

Customs procedure was virtually waived. Perhaps the sickness had been well worth while! Besides, La Segovia had now reached the building and was well into the process of her entry. Voices gabbled. The scene was one of milling figures and popping bulbs. *Flash, flash, flash....' Acá, La Segovia! Una sonrisa! —ya, ya!'*

And Segovia herself: 'Darlings, darlings, I love you all! No, please *don't* photograph from that side!'

Dumbly, Barry stood alone now. He was in the dusty hall, outside of the final barrier, watching Segovia as she laughed and shrilled through the swinging glass doors into what he imagined was a V.I.P. lounge. More champagne, more brandy—or so he supposed; he'd had more than enough of that, but by Jesus he was through. Safe. That was what counted. New identity. New life.

'Good evening,' said a voice at his elbow. 'Mr. Kegan, isn't it? Barry Kegan? I thought you were up for life.'

Barry's scalp crawled. Instinctively he protested, 'No, I'm afraid you're mistaken. The name's Martinson.'

'Ah, that'll be what you call yourself now. We both know different. My name's Gareth Davies, it's my real name. U.N.F. Syndication. You may have seen my by-line from time to time.'

Davies' speech had a faintly Welsh lilt. He looked somewhat like a rubicund gnome with heavy glasses and a bristling crest of red hair. A shave may have improved his appearance.

'I'm sorry.' Wheeling to go, just as a uniformed immigration man crossed the hall, Barry caught himself in check. Davies' hand closed persistently on his elbow.

'No mistake, Mr. Kegan.'

Barry's voice, against his own will, lifted ringingly. 'Shut up, shut up you Gaelic twat! If you call me that just one more time I'll push your nose clean through to the back of your neck.'

'It's been done before.' Davies merely grinned.

'You should know better than to intimidate the press. We can make things very uncomfortable. Why not talk things over in my car? I'll run you into Ciudad Felice. Much better than the airport coach. That won't depart for at least an hour. No telling how many of the boys will have got you spotted by then, eh?'

'Aren't you here to cover Segovia?'

'I've got something better now. Listen. "Escaped lifer arrives in San Felice"? How's that for a catch line?'

'It isn't true.'

'Then you'll get a free ride to your hotel with no obligations. We'll talk on the way. Nice and private. You'll be able to convince me. Now, let me help you with these cases.'

Half stupefied, Barry gave in. He was still not feeling well. Besides, into his memory had flashed the wildest conviction—that possibly this peppery, expatriate Welsh gnome was the contact man he had been promised. The more he thought, the likelier it seemed.

They pulled thankfully away from the flagged bay, away from sodium lights, into open country. The road was hedged with spiny cactus grovelling for a hold in baked earth. The windows were down, and an acrid smelling breeze came in from across the cane fields.

'I congratulate you on your escape,' Davies opened pleasantly. 'The hospital wing, wasn't it? But you never managed it alone. I know that much.'

'I don't care what you *think* you know.'

'A really professional job. Must have cost a bomb to organize....' Davies' head swivelled sharply to stare.

Kegan said, 'You know what it's like in stir? Altogether, I've done twelve years. No matter what happens, I can't do any more. I'll kill you before you get a chance to turn me in.'

Davies coughed roupily, spat through the open window, and effected a noisy gear change.

'Talk sense, man.'

'I've already killed once. It was easy.'

'A bloody accident; accidents always are easy. The security guard lost his head. Both of you panicked. There's a difference between cold blooded murder and a man getting killed in a struggle for a loaded gun.'

Restlessly, Kegan shuffled his feet. 'Bastards like you dug my grave with pencils. Now you want to dig it all over again.'

'No, listen, boyo. Papers report facts.'

'They slant them, twist them, turn them inside out, then extract a significance that was never intended from the most casual remark.'

'You're getting the sub editorials mixed up with learned counsel.' Davies uttered a wry chuckle. 'Careful. There's precious little love to be found between those two. In a manner of speaking, they're in the same business. Forget about them.'

Slowly, Barry became aware that he had made a terrible error of judgement. This man was not his contact.

'You know the hell of a lot about me,' he said warily.

'Eight years ago, I covered your trial at the Old Bailey. Sure I know you. University graduate turned black sheep.' Davies grunted. 'Know what? A prize fool, that's you, not a bloody murderer. Five years of my life I'd give, to have had half your chances. And you chuck the lot away for a sharp course in blowing safes ... Look what it's got you.'

'What did University get me? A three-year course of nothing, plus a set of values I can never afford. And the opportunity to develop a natural talent for thieving.'

'Oh, come off it, boyo. Another minute and you'll have me crying in the beer ... you're safe enough now. Well, I mean to say. No treaty of extradition between Britain and San Felice; so it's business by polite request, and I can't see the President agreeing to extradition in your case. Ricardo Torres ... up at University together, weren't you? So you're counting on the Old Pal's act for asylum. Can't blame you for that.' Angrily, Davies tugged the wheel around a hairpin bend. The ground was rising, pitted and uneven. They lumped up the incline among scattered tamarisks and umbrella pines, past a citrus orchard and the first outlying houses. Cracked and drab, their sombre uniformity was relieved only by occasional flares of poinsettia and clematis. The heat was oppressive.

Barry kept silent. His immediate concern went no farther than the prospect of a bath and sleep; but Davies' revelations had shaken him deeply.

The press man ground savagely, 'All right. Some of you people get it ready made, and others, like me, have to fight for every penny. But don't start feeling too secure. The country's overdue for revolution. These South American republics aren't noted for their stability. Remember that it's Torres who'll be first to get the chop, and that's the reason why I happen to be on the scene. Our Man on the Spot, bye-line San Felice. But I'm not averse to a God-given exclusive while I wait for the political situation to hot up.'

'An exclusive from me? I'll see you in hell first.'

'Three thousand any good?'

'Pesos?'

'Quid.'

'You're taking the piss.'

Davies flicked at his spectacles with an irritable movement of one hand.

'Five thousand. Make it an expensive piss. Tax free.'

'Stuff it. What exactly are you buying, anyway?'

'Everything. Including the gang who sprung you, how they did it—the lot. You needn't mention names. I'll want your picture; and your signature on each leaf of my copy.'

'The last thing I signed bounced pretty high.'

'Let's stop fencing, Mr. Kegan, and start talking sense. There are plenty of places to get lost in South America. Hiding is a national pastime. Five thousand quid will hide you in comfort for quite a long while. Give the hoo-hah chance to die down....' Davies' nicotine stained fingers drummed on the wheel rim. 'With a story like yours, you won't escape the other news boys for long. So if it's not me, it'll be someone else. Sign up now and be done with them.'

'For Christ's...' Trailing off, Kegan turned his head away. 'Give me a break.'

'Which hotel? We're almost in town.'

'I'm expected at the *Fortuna*.'

'Okay. Sleep on it. I know you're tired....' Davies bared his teeth; his early confidence had started to slip. He was getting desperate. 'I'll come back tomorrow for your answer.'

More from sheer relief than acquiescence, Kegan yielded a nod. They lapsed into silence.

This was the capital, Ciudad Felice. Its tree-lined avenues were sepulchrally still in the moonlight, ochreous façades a ghostly shade of grey. The car drummed past fountains, gaseosa stalls, statues of past Presidents, while the figure of a sentry with a steel helmet and fixed bayonet stood rigidly at every crossroads like a human bookmark.

The *Hotel Fortuna* lay in a square off the main avenue. In the centre of the square a circle of brown grass bristled with moth-eaten dwarf palms and long stemmed light globes.

A night clerk with a droopy moustache, discoloured as if by snuff, greeted Kegan at the reception desk. Yes, a room had been reserved. Sign here, please. Passport? Gracias. The room key: here it is, come this way....

Barry heard it through a fog of sleep.

In the rumbling lift, the clerk asked, 'For how long will you be staying, señor?'

Kegan blinked feebly. He didn't know for sure, but the clerk seemed indifferent: mañana, tomorrow would do.

Barry waited until the door of the room closed, isolating him within its faded decor; but it was clean, and the bed looked a damned sight more comfortable than the ones he'd grown accustomed to these last eight years. A kiosk-sized shower cubicle with a torn plastic curtain reminded how sticky and uncomfortable he was.

The cases were thrown on the bed. He began to strip off his clothes. When he did so, he discovered the brown-wrapped package that Segovia had persuaded him to smuggle through customs.... He rasped a humourless laugh. *Persuaded?* Got him maudlin-drunk, more like it, only now the laugh was on her.

Kegan sized up the package, hefted it, shook it beside his ear. Something inside rattled hollowly. After a moment he shrugged, ripped off the paper, then set down the box on his bedside table before drawing a profound breath. Solid ivory with a filigree gold inlay, if he knew anything. The lousy, syphilitic cow! No wonder she had preferred someone else to take the chances! Viciously, he unfastened the catch and raised the lid. Then he became really dazed. A jewel box complete with Swiss musical action and a tiny ballerina dancing to the tinny notes of *La Ronde*, but it was the contents that really caused his head to swim. Emeralds, rubies, gold clasps: even his estimated value was more than enough to stun him.

Then he began to laugh. He had to check himself from hysteria; this was really too rich for credence. A thief's wildest dreams come true. If the stuff wasn't paste, his worries were over once and for all, completely over!

But now that his weariness had magically fled, everything was being replaced by the crazy, headlong panic that screamed at him to get the hell out of this place: out, out, and soon, as soon as he'd had a shower and time to think.

Still inclined to giggle, Kegan undressed and slid under the cold-needle spray. *La Ronde* ran itself to a standstill, but almost as the last notes died away, the silence was broken again—this time by a thunderous banging at the door.

'Open up! Open the door! It is the police!'

... Time must have elapsed, how long he couldn't know; but before he could collect his wits, a key had turned in the lock. Emerging from the shower, shoulders beaded with water, Kegan glimpsed the terrified figure of the night clerk hovering in the background.

Inside the room were two men; one was a uniformed inspector, the peak of his cap embossed with braid. The other wore plain clothes, pure, lightweight linen, patterned shoes. He was paunchy and baggy-eyed, with a mere point of a beard, and oddly familiar.

'You're not the police,' Kegan addressed him nonsensically, playing for time. Fury paralysed his thinking. All he felt was a sense of absurdity, standing there bare-arsed and helpless.

'On the contrary, Mr. Kegan,' the words came icily, 'I'm a very special kind of policeman. My business is security.'

Kegan. The name engendered in Barry a tide of self vilification which was futile now. It did no good, but he couldn't help that. Davies must have shopped him. *Oh, that Welsh grass, that utter bastard!*

'Ephraim Caldes.' The security man bowed. He was collected, suave, almost bored. The scene might have been one he had witnessed many times, one that he watched merely for studying the victim's reaction to stress.

Caldes picked up the jewel box and began to wind the musical action. He let it run.

'Charming.... We know all about you, Mr. Kegan. We know you're a professional thief. You've entered San Felice under false credentials ... I'm afraid, with the charges we have against you, you can expect little help from your embassy. You don't mind telling me how you obtained this little toy?'

'Believe it or not, it was given to me by Nana Segovia. She gulled me into carrying it through the customs—'

'She *what*?' Caldes looked amused. 'How odd, then, that she should have reported it stolen, and by a man named Martinson.'

'Now, just hold everything—'

Standing there, Kegan glimpsed his own pallid nudity in the reflection darkness had created in the window.

'Go on, Mr. Kegan.'

'That's not my name.'

'I'm afraid that we know it is. Also that Miss Segovia befriended you in the course of a long and tedious journey, wined you and dined you extravagantly, and in return for her generosity you robbed her.'

'She framed me, that fat, dirty—'

'Stop!' Caldes' polished-agate eyes took on a glisten that was intimidating. 'Be very careful how you describe one of our most cherished national figures. And explain to me why Nana Segovia should want to frame a most unpleasant thief and convicted murderer like you? As you say in your language, what's in it for her? You gulled her into believing you to be a thorough gentleman, that's the measure of her generosity. She couldn't believe you had stolen from her.'

A tiny quirk dipped the corners of Caldes' lips. He had slanted, Indian eyes and broad nostrils that flattened when he smiled. He plucked a top sheet from the bed and flung it across to Kegan.

'You are under arrest. Wrap that around you. Or would you prefer to be handcuffed?'

Outside, the big police car stood black and shining. Across the square Kegan noticed a huge, florid face on a poster hoarding that had been partially disfigured and splashed with mud. TORRES, SI! TORRES, VIVA! It was an old poster. Ricardo's familiar features seemed even older.

Barry hesitated.

'Where are you taking me?'

'To the police station, naturally, to be charged.'

Before getting into the car, Kegan took one more glance at that face on the hoarding. He wondered silently what the charge would be if Caldes were to learn that he, Barry Kegan, had come to San Felice for the sole purpose of killing their President.

Chapter Two

THE PRISONER

Chafed by rough blankets, his body seemed intolerably heavy. Time after time he re-lived the events of the last three weeks, wanting only sleep, while his mind went back to the moment of that jarring drop from the prison wall. *Up, get up; across the road— there's the car!*

The engine refused to start; the battery was clapped. No death this cruel, the horrible knowledge that escape rested upon inert coils of wire and twelve rotten cells that wouldn't feed a charge.

'Under this rug, mate! Keep your ruddy nut down!'

Jolt, jolt: the car fired at last then picked up, still without alarm from the black prison walls behind, and moved away sluggishly.

'How do you feel now?'

'Ill.' Kegan groaned weakly. 'I don't know what was in that blasted pill you slipped me, but I've been sicker than a dog for twenty-four hours.'

'A *free* dog, mate. Don't forget it.' *Chuckle.* Somebody, God only knew who, was enjoying a good laugh at Barry Kegan's expense. 'Suffering's said to be good for the soul. That pill shunted you into the hospital where you wanted to be: that's all that matters, see?'

'The doctor diagnosed gastro enteritis. Another day like yesterday and he'd have had me in Hammersmith General. Does Billy Spinks always cut things this fine?'

'Never mind, you're out. Everything go to plan?'

'Along the corridor,' Kegan said. 'Out of the window and across the yard. But, Jesus, my guts! Try climbing a rope in my condition, and in pyjamas at that. See how you like it.'

Another chuckle; this time a different voice.

'Socks and shoes under the rug. Got 'em? Now nut down!—Copper on the corner of Broadway.'

Under the smothering rug, Barry warmed up rapidly; but his insides were a running tide-wash of pain. If they didn't get him to a lavatory soon he was going to be in trouble. The car's bumpy motion was doing nothing to help.

'You still all right?' A hand shook him.

Kegan managed, 'Just about. Where are we going?'

'Straight to Billy Spinks. You haven't met Billy yet. There's a lot he wants to tell you.'

'I've a few things to say, too. Mostly concerning the pills he dishes out.' Barry had subsided. He wasn't interested in Billy Spinks, only in getting away, but unfortunately men like Spinks were a part of that.

They were still travelling when the car radio broke out with the news of Kegan's escape. Even then, Barry had lost interest in that phase of events; but he couldn't shut out the hoarse voices from the front seats.

'Watching the ports, are they? What a ruddy hope! I ask you!'

Click. The radio went off; now there was only the swish of tyres. Kegan gritted his teeth, tried to sleep, but the cramping belly pains wouldn't let him get comfortable.

When he finally went in to meet Spinks, about two hours later, the pains were beginning to lessen. It was his temper that grew frayed now. And his first impression of Spinks did little to improve it. Billy Spinks looked deceptively mild and very, very Jewish.

Marooned in an island of light in an otherwise pitch-dark room, he sat at a desk, sleeves above his skinny forearms, motionless as a crouching cat waiting for the mouse to come nearer. Upon the desk rested a pistol, its butt cross-hatched in rich brown.

'How do you feel, Barry boy?'

'Rotten.'

'All that will clear up in a day. Within forty-eight hours you'll be on your way to the coast. A launch will whip you across to the French coast, then you'll go by car to Paris and pick up a scheduled flight to Mexico City. Any questions?'

'Yes. What do I have to do in return?'

Lazily, Spinks moved at last. He scratched one side of his nose.

'I'm very glad you asked me that. It was part of the deal, wasn't it, that you did a little job for me? I hate people who welsh on their debts. Don't you?'

'I pay mine.'

Somewhere from the enclosing darkness, a soft laugh. Spinks shifted the anglepoise lamp so that it shone directly into Kegan's eyes.

'Good. Now sit down while I tell you all about it.'

'Can't it wait?'

'Could you wait to get out of the nick? Sit down.' He snapped his fingers. A chair was thrust into view.

Barry sat down. Now that his eyes were growing accustomed to the gloom, he made out the form of another man, a bulk among shadows less black, sitting just behind Spinks. A pair of trousered legs were loosely crossed, the knuckles of a hand resting upon the knee. The first finger lacked its top joint.

Kegan became aware of a cloying scent, quite unmistakable; somebody in the room was sucking peppermint.

'Straight to the point,' Spinks said. 'Remember back to University. You were friendly with a boy named Torres.'

'We spent a year together at the Sorbonne.'

'Right. You had ideas of a diplomatic career.'

'Ideals, not ideas. Ricardo Torres became President of his home Republic of San Felice. You know all this, but what's it got to do with me?'

'You have to go in and kill Torres. Do that, then we're quits.'

The unexpectedness of it took a long while to sink in. Kegan could scarcely believe his ears.

'Assassination? Why me?'

'A question of pulling a trigger. You've done that before, haven't you? It's nothing new. Besides,' and Spinks snapped his fingers decisively, 'this is one trigger only you can pull. Torres is too well guarded to be reached by just anyone. There have been plenty of attempts.'

'Threatened men live long,' Kegan grunted.

'Not too long,' Spinks remarked. 'It's up to you to pull the old school tie act on Torres. And don't ask me questions. Did I ask questions when you made it known you wanted to be sprung, and at any price? People come to me and ask me to do them a job.

They're customers. I take my money and scarper, just as you will, but you can think it over if you like. Take five minutes. Who's in any hurry?'

Spinks picked up the gun and toyed with it. That was the point at which Kegan's mind jittered away and yanked him back to his filthy little cell in Ciudad Felice. He was virtually back to where he had started; he had merely exchanged cells, and this time there was no Spinks to spring him.

At some point during the night he must have fallen asleep, for suddenly it was broad daylight. As his gaze broke away, a lizard travelled across one wall like a spurt of green flame and vanished over the window ledge.

Barry sat up. The fatigue had vanished, but the hatred of how Spinks had let him down festered in his mind. There should have been a contact at the airport; somebody to take him in hand and light the way, and at first, stupidly, he had suspected that person to be Gareth Davies. Hell!

He should have waited for the airport bus. Couldn't even really blame Spinks for what had happened—nobody could have counted on Nana Segovia; she was just one of those imponderables.

Two stoical constables fetched him a breakfast tray. Uninterested in the food, Kegan watched them without stirring; his clothing was tossed on the foot of the bed.

'Get dressed.'

'What for?'

Kegan received no answer. The door banged shut.

The cell was too quiet. Traffic noises that filtered in were muted by distance, but the heat was gradually worsening. He could see through the barred window to where a mop-headed palm waved coyly over the top of the wall, and the sky was a cloudless blue. Free of clouds. Free.

He got off the bed, walked to the grey, scum grimed hand basin, and turned the faucet. A dribble of tepid, rusty water trickled out. There wasn't any soap.

He sniffed at the porridge, revolted by the smell. The bread was dry, and he nibbled at it tastelessly for a while; doing this helped to pass the time, how much of it he had no idea. They hadn't let him keep his watch.

Kegan was dozing when Ephraim Caldes arrived.

'Get up.'

'Why?'

'Don't argue. Do as you're told.'

After a moment, Barry stood on his feet. One of the guards advanced and snapped a pair of handcuffs on his wrists.

'What's this, then? Arraignment for trial?'

Caldes himself looked washed out. The shadows under his eyes were dark smudges. His lips were pinched and quivering. In a low voice, he said: 'You really are a most fortunate man. The President of this republic has asked to meet you. Until he does, you will be treated exactly the same as any other prisoner.'

Barry had the sensation of being caught in a web from which there was absolutely no escape. He could hardly believe it was all happening.

*   *   *

Through the centre of Ciudad Felice the police

driver flicked on the car siren, clearing the traffic and making Kegan feel like some magnificent felon on his way to the guillotine.

Plazas, streets, and buildings, quivered in the brutal noonday heat. Down a long avenida lined with trees, people sat outside cafés under canvas awnings.

The car screamed past clanking trams, out of the town and across a bridge that spanned a mere trickle of water. Off to one side a majestic white building stood well back from the riverbank, surrounded by wrought iron fencing which was patrolled by sentries. Overhead the tricoloured flag of San Felice floated restlessly in the heat tormented air.

'Presidential Palace,' Caldes informed, without further comment. He seemed disinclined for conversation of any sort.

Barry decided that he had gone far enough.

'Last night my cigarettes were taken. May I have one to smoke now?' He added, 'Please.'

Ephraim Caldes stirred.

'I loathe and detest the very smell of tobacco.' He spoke with a tart snap, then fumbled in his pocket. 'Here. Have one of these instead.'

A tube of peppermints. Automatically Kegan took one ... took it, sucked at it, and then grew suddenly cold. His brain cast back yet again to Billy Spinks and a darkened room in the south of London. The pungent odour of peppermint; a dimly seen figure in the shadows at Spinks' elbow; it all added up to one big, sinister query.

Without trying to make himself too obvious, Barry strained for a glimpse of Caldes' hands. What he saw only affirmed the query; Caldes' left index finger was missing its top joint.

Mentally, Kegan collapsed, wondering what he should do and now positive that this was the contact man of whom Spinks had talked. He was puzzled by Caldes' way of handling the whole affair; but that was none of his business. He could guess the rest. Intrigue in high places! But it all fell neatly into place. Too neatly, perhaps.

Open country lay ahead with hills skirting the horizon, sandy against the sky but tenuous like phantom clouds veined white and purple.

Work had ceased in the fields. Here and there, rows of scarecrow labourers dozed in the shade under vast straw hats, none of them moving as the car rumbled past.

Closer to the hills the country turned green, with occasional clusters of palm trees around adobe-walled hovels. A grove of acacia and whispering poplars lifted out of the landscape, in the centre of them an unbearably white villa encircled with its own high wall.

Here, a narrow road bore off the main highway and dived beneath sheltering trees, a green-cool oasis in a sea of shimmering heat.

There was a military roadblock manned by soldiers in grey—grey shirts, grey forage caps with yellow piping—with automatic rifles. The car stopped yards short of their roadblock, and out of the low brick guardhouse emerged an officer-figure wearing dark glasses. He approached and saluted.

Caldes, leaning across, unfastened Barry's handcuffs and motioned him out.

'I am handing you over to the officer of the guard,' he said. 'Do not think that we are parting for the last time. We shall meet again. Make no mistake.'

Sitting back, he slammed the door of the car.

The officer in grey saluted Barry yet again.

'Señor Kegan? Welcome to the Villa Santa Cruz. If you would accompany me?'

He had a brown face and white smile. Young, too; and not a typical Feliciano.

Kegan was seized by a wild premonition that somehow he had stumbled over a borderline and was lost in the hinterlands of fantasy. The sentry of the gate sprang to attention and smacked one hand to the butt of his rifle as they passed into the grounds of the villa where a fountain tinkled away in the centre of velvet smooth lawns.

The paved avenues wheel-spoked out through acres of flowering shrubbery. There were arched walks under clematis-bearing trellis; everything seemed to have a delicate, sensuous perfume, and further off, Kegan saw a sprinkler swirling the water in eccentric patterns over a miniature putting green.

The pathway skirted a clump of red-flowering bushes and Kegan came into sight of the villa once again, its veranda shaded under masses of jasmine and smelling of frangipane, where a man and a woman were having afternoon tea. China-ware tinkled, cutlery flashed the reflected sunlight, a woman's voice laughed.

Kegan's fantasy sensation was increased. The vicar's Sunday tea party, he thought; now he really knew he'd gone over the edge. One of the figures looked up, then got to his feet: the man, slender, still young, but prematurely grey at the temples. He did not at all resemble his likeness on that poster Barry had seen the night before.

'Barry Kegan! Come and sit down, you old...!'

As if this was the last shock his wire-strung nerves could withstand, Kegan found himself shaking. He extended his hand ... smack! Solid flesh; he half expected the other hand to disintegrate.

Torres flung one arm around his shoulders and hugged him solidly.

'Barry, I could scarcely believe it when Ephraim told me you were in San Felice. I understand you've got yourself involved in some ghastly mix-up.'

'I'm surprised he admitted it was a mix-up.'

'Well, don't worry. We'll get it sorted out....' Torres laughed outright. 'Now come over here. I want you to meet Rojas.'

Barry reacted to his first real sight of Rojas Modesta. She had that certain ripeness of body so common among Latin girls, although she was no longer teenaged. She had black hair worn European style. Kegan took her hand, the bones small and light like those of a bird, and yet she wasn't fragile. He hated fragile women.

'English tea is served, Barry.' Torres grinned. 'Rojas, do the honours.'

She poured some tea into the cup she had used herself and watched Barry under her dark lashes.

Torres demanded irritably, 'En que consiste, Rojas?'

'It's all right,' Kegan put in.

'No, Barry, it is not all right. She's playing her little games. This one happens to be called, embarrass the president's guest. And one day she'll go too far.'

Rojas uncrossed her legs with a faint whisper, got to her feet, and smiled languidly. 'You would like a clean cup, Señor Kegan? Or would you prefer iced beer?'

'Beer,' he said. 'Please.'

Rojas walked with a sway to her hips which made Kegan aware once again that it was years since he had known a woman. But a second later his interest was stifled by alarm.

She had paused to call in a high, shrill hissing manner between her teeth, in response to which something moved in the shadows at one side of the veranda. At first Kegan thought it must be a dog—a very big one.

'Angelito! Aqui, hijo!'

The jaguar shook itself. It paced across a bar of sunlight, pausing to stretch and yawn. Fully grown, it resembled a gigantic tabby with high-arched rump and head down, forelegs extended to strop unsheathed claws across the floor.

'Angelito!'

A note of impatience. Rojas slapped her thigh and the big cat padded up to her.

'Our guests rarely pay a second visit,' Torres remarked. 'You can see why.... What did you think of Rojas? We must seem ill mannered, the way we bicker, but don't let that deceive you.'

'It doesn't. The only thing that shakes me is how an old ram like you ever managed to find a girl like that!'

'Still after my women?' There was a barb in Torres' voice although they were bantering, but it gave Kegan a feeling of security. He listened and smiled.

'When I first met Rojas, she was a fashion model—not a very good one, her statistics were basically wrong. Not tall enough or skinny enough. Then she won the Miss Latin America contest, had minor parts in a few rotten Mexican films ... and she was glad to retire from all that. Enough about us, Barry, how have *you* been keeping all these years?'

'Caldes didn't tell you? I've been a bad boy and now I'm on the run—over the hills and far away.'

Torres played with a spoon, clinking it against the side of his cup.

'You don't need to say more.' His shoulders changed position with the merest hint of a shrug.

Before Kegan could reply, Rojas reappeared with the beer. Over the frosted bottles, the wisps of vapour lingered, and Barry downed a good third of his glass at a gulp.

Rojas said, 'I tend to bore Ricardo. I hope you're doing better; San Felice is a boring place.'

'Barry's here to stay for as long as he wishes. Get himself sorted out.' Ricardo Torres paused. 'Later,' speaking in a dry-leaf rustle, 'he *may* find life a little repetitive.'

Rojas laughed, 'Why not tell him the truth? No, don't. I'll tell it.' She wheeled round on Kegan. 'I'm a prisoner. We both are. So you will be.'

Barry could deal with this. 'I'm afraid,' he told her, 'you have no idea what being a real prisoner is like. That's something I'm certain I know far better than you.'

'Touché,' said Torres. 'But don't start off by quarrelling, you two.' He caught both their hands. 'Only two people I can trust; I don't want any little squabbles.' He stopped, but only to wink at Kegan. 'I can see you're done in. I took the liberty of having your bags sent out this morning. You want to get cleaned up now?'

'I could use a bath.'

'Right, I'll hand you over to Potts. Potts is a gentleman's gentleman, Barry, and I'm certain you're going to be amazed. I'll ask you later what you think of him!'

*   *   *

Henry Irving Potts dressed remarkably like Arthur Treacher in his Hollywood heyday; striped trousers, tuxedo jacket, hand tied bow.

'May I run you a bath, sir?'

'I'd prefer to run it myself.'

'Just as you wish, sir.' A slightly pained expression crossed Potts' face. 'In that case, I'll unpack your bags.'

'Leave them.' Kegan, locating the bags at his bedside, asked softly, 'You are English, aren't you?'

'Decidedly.'

'And I take it you're well looked after here?'

'Quite so, sir.'

Potts had a rich, plummy voice and a disconcerting manner of looking as if from a great height, which grated on Kegan's nerves.

'Is it a prerequisite of this job, Potts?'

'Is what, sir?' Potts became ill at ease.

'You're laying on the grand manner with a trowel.' Kegan showed his teeth, but he wasn't smiling. 'How much bird have you done?'

Potts jumped, puffed like a stranded fish, and for a second lost his composure. He threw a startled glance in the direction of the dark-skinned Feliciano maid busy straightening the bed linen.

'What?'

'You forgot to say "sir".'

'I'm afraid—'

'And you talk from one side of your mouth. Your eyes shift whenever anyone passes behind your range of vision.... Does that girl understand English?'

'Thank heavens, no. And President Torres is fully aware of my unfortunate ... er ...'

'Oh, stop being so humble! As a matter of interest, how did you manage to achieve...' Barry gestured helplessly, 'all this? The voice, the dress, the fancy manner?'

Still without any perceptible change of expression, Potts lowered one eyelid.

'A trade secret which took me half a lifetime to discover. Everything is written down in books which can be had from a library at no charge.'

A balloon-like swell of laughter erupted under Kegan's ribs. 'Well, tone it down a bit, Potts, tone it down!'

He was sitting on the edge of the bed, kicking off his shoes. His sweltering feet expanded in the cool air. Nearby, the maid had drawn the curtains to relieve the furnace blast outside and cool the interior even further.

Kegan could not resist asking, 'And what do you do for recreation, if it's not too rude a question?'

'Spend an evening in Ciudad Felice once a week. I have my own transport, a motorized cycle.'

It conjured quite a spectacle, Kegan thought, Potts in striped pants and bowler hat batting across the dusty roads to the amusement of the paisanos.

The Feliciano girl curtseyed, hands clasped in front of her, waiting to be dismissed. Potts inclined his head slightly.

'Recreation, sir? No lack of that.'

As the girl passed him he brought down the flat of his hand, with a crisp smack, upon her high provocative bottom.

'Will that be all, sir?' Potts asked, without the quiver of an eyelash. 'I draw your attention to the service bell at your bedside. And I would advise you to make use of the mosquito netting at night.'

Kegan grinned. 'Very good, Potts.'

'Oh!' Half-way across the threshold, Potts checked and affirmed, 'Dinner, sir, at eight.'

Noiselessly he closed the door, leaving Kegan to run both hands over his glistening face before starting to unpack the cases. The stubble around his chin needed the attentions of a razor, but he got no further in his search than the top layer of clothing before he came to the gun. It was heavy, the butt rich brown; the same kind of weapon he had seen before, lying on a desk in front of Billy Spinks.

Barry picked it up, then let it fall to the bed. There was something else in that case, besides the gun: a thick wad of notes. As if Spinks had materialized at his elbow, Kegan heard the slurred Jewish tones. 'Your contact in San Felice will handle everything— including your getaway afterwards. Wait until he tells you when to act. It won't be long. All you'll have to do is pull that trigger. But a month from now, Torres is going to be dead ... *or you will be*.' His heart hammer-pounding, Kegan advanced to the window and threw aside the curtains. The room had grown choking with menace.

He unfastened the casements, leaning out to gulp the clean air. Blinking his heavy eyes he stared across to the veranda where Torres and Rojas sat talking quietly. Ricardo had his back towards the window and Kegan thought wildly, *I couldn't miss, not from this range. He might hear the shot, but he'd never know what hit him.*

Kegan knew, and had known all along, that this execution would never be accomplished. It was beyond him even if he'd wanted to go through with it. To hell with Spinks. Bloody hell with him. Spinks was thousands of miles away. What could he do? Kegan started unbuttoning his shirt, then he stopped.

Wherever Spinks may be, whatever he could do or could not do in London, Ephraim Caldes was in Ciudad Felice. Caldes was a different proposition. There was absolutely no telling what Caldes might do.

The parting words came back with a chilling atmosphere of evil...

'We shall meet again. Make no mistake.'

Chapter Three

THE CLEOPATRA SYNDROME

Kegan awoke to find the white tuxedo neatly arranged on his bedside chair. Must be one of Ricardo's, he assumed, recalling the old days when they had swapped their combined assets indiscriminately.... Identical sizes in everything including women.

Barry dressed feeling pleasantly hungry and went downstairs to find dinner.

It was quite dark by now; he could hear the fountain's musical tinkle above a million cicadas.

Torres was alone at the rail of the veranda, smoking a cigar, staring at the night with the fixedness of a man seeing mirages. Nearby, the jaguar was spread at Rojas' feet, raising its head with a tail-twitch and a deep grumble as Kegan approached.

Torres turned and smiled, 'Barry! Now you look civilized! I see that our clothes are still interchangeable.'

But Kegan's attention went first to Rojas. The pearls at her throat were magnificently offset by her dark-tanned throat and shoulders.

At the table, a picture of white damask, silverware and candles, Potts withdrew the wine from its silver ice bucket and filled the three glasses.

'While you've been recharging the batteries,' Torres informed, 'I've been getting some pretty angry phone calls from your consular people. The ambassador seems to take my reception of you as a personal affront. You have no idea what an uproar you've become in the national press.'

Kegan abruptly lost his appetite. 'They want me handed over, do they? So I'm causing you a lot of trouble.'

Torres smiled faintly, but his grey-speckled eyes were grave.

'Don't call it trouble. I'm telling you this because I have a solution in mind, but you can credit Rojas with the idea.'

He was hesitant before committing to words something that might offend, and glanced at Rojas as if for reassurance.

'The fact is that we might cause a minor splash in diplomatic circles, but what Britain can do to me, or to San Felice rather, is precisely nothing. Even although we share no treaty to cover a situation like this one, form's the thing, and the worst that can happen is that I'm looked upon as a bit of a bounder. It's fortunate in a way that I'm able to refuse on the grounds that you're being held to answer offences against the laws of this state. What Rojas proposes, and I can't imagine why I never thought of it first, is that you could apply to become a citizen. See what I mean? It sows everything up tight in spite of the fact that your ambassador will be fully aware there's been some jiggery pokery.'

'It will save his face in London,' Kegan said. 'This change of nationality. Can it be done?'

'I can't see why not, but don't be too hasty. You'll want time to think.'

Kegan laughed hollowly. 'Going back to Britain's

out of the question, first because I'd be re-arrested and second because I have to earn a living somehow. And the only thing I really understand is a locked safe.'

Torres flexed his hands; he wrung a sagging grin.

'We have one here that I use for top security documents. The manufacturers insist it's burglar proof.'

'That kind are my speciality. You see, Ricky, I'm just not a desirable citizen.'

Torres' features straightened. 'With an education like yours? .... Hell, educated people are scarce out here. My economists, for example; no more than bloody amateurs. Once your papers come through, we'll find you something. The Administration can stand all the brain it can get.'

'So now I'm part of the brain drain? Quite a thought!'

Torres punched his shoulder affectionately. They ate, Kegan watching Rojas from the corner of his eye. He couldn't help it. Once he caught her attention, but it was impossible to make out how she was taking it. Certainly she had understood everything that was being said, even if she took little part in it. Her command of English was immaculate.

They retired to easy chairs at the far end of the veranda. Angelito, outspread a few inches from Kegan's feet, blinked intermittently with his chin resting along the floor.

Rojas extended her arm to curry-comb the big velvety ears with her finger tips.

'Angelito makes you nervous? There's no need. Provided you keep every action slow and leisurely, give him plenty of time to see what's going on, you can do what you like in perfect safety.'